AF265751

THE FIRST ANNUAL DUCK SPRINGS WHISTLING CONTEST

ReadersMagnet, LLC

BOBBIE J. MCLAREN

DEDICATION

I would like to dedicate this book to my two favorite great-nephews.

You both inspire me.

"1ST"
FIRST ANNUAL
DUCK SPRINGS
WHISTLING CONTEST
TO BE IN
CITY PARK
MAY 28TH
THREE AGE GROUPS WITH
PRIZES FOR EACH YEARS
5-7 YEARS
8-10 YEARS
11-12 YEARS
GRAND PRIZE $100.00
INQUIRE INSIDE

Duck Springs was covered with the notices of the big event that was to soon take place. The contest was open to all children between the ages of 5 and 12 years old. The busiest place in town was Johnson's General Store on Main Street.

"1ST"
FIRST ANNUAL
DUCK SPRINGS
WHISTLING CONTEST

TO BE IN
CITY PARK
MAY 28TH

THREE AGE GROUPS WITH PRIZES FOR EACH YEARS

5-7 YEARS
8-10 YEARS
11-12 YEARS

GRAND PRIZE $50.00

The reason was because in the front window hung three sterling silver whistles to be awarded to the First Place winners in each of the three age groups; 5-7 years, 8-10 years and 11-12 years old. The Grand Prize Winner would be chosen from one of the three first place winners and they would receive an additional prize of a $50.00 gift card.

BRANDON

"Dad, I just cleaned that window and now look at it!" Brandon Johnson said wearily. Brandon was 14 years old with wavy brown hair and freckles. He worked weekends to help his dad and to earn money for the summer.

"Well son," Mr. Johnson replied, "I know you've had to redo that window every hour, but it's only for a couple more weeks". As Brandon picked up the window cleaner, his eyes fell on the many hand and face prints on the glass. Stepping outside, Brandon spotted Tyler James gazing in the window.

"Hey! Get your hands off that glass," Brandon growled as he neared Tyler, "Don't you see that mess you're making?"

"I'm sorry, Brandon," Tyler sheepishly said as his big brown eyes began to tear. "Aw, you didn't do all that by yourself," Brandon said as he tousled Tyler's sandy blond hair. "I guess I'm just tired of cleaning that window."

CONTESTANT ENTRY
1st Annual
Duck Spring
whistling
Contest
NAME
PARENT
DATE
EMAIL
MAY 28

"I'll try to keep my hands off of it." "Thanks. Hey, are you entering the contest?" Instantly a smile spread across Tyler's face and his eyes sparkled with excitement. "My mom is picking up the entry form today!"

As Brandon wiped off the last of the prints, he looked down at Tyler and asked, "How old are you?" "Six!!" beamed Tyler, "And I'm going to beat everyone and win that whistle!" "Well, since I'm too old to enter, I'll be cheering for you." "Thanks Brandon."

"Tyler!" his mother called, "Come on, we have to go." Waving goodbye he ran to catch up to his mom.

For the next two weeks you could hear whistling everywhere you went in Duck Springs. Many of the parents had begun to hide small amounts of cotton in their ears to help them survive the never ending shrill. Each child trained daily to improve their sound. Yet none worked any harder than Tyler. He whistled at home, at school and wherever he went.

A B
C
1 2 3

"Tyler James!" Miss Perkins snapped, "Stop that whistling right this minute, or I'll have to send you to Mr.Carp." "Yes ma'am," he respectfully replied, since he sure didn't want to go to the principal's office. But still he ran the song he was planning to whistle through his head and imagined how wonderful it was going to sound.

Even in his sleep, he dreamed of that shiny silver whistle that would be his when he won. He didn't think 'if' he would win, because he only planned to win.

On the last day of school before the big day of the contest, Tyler was riding his scooter the one block home, when suddenly mean Billy Carp, the principal's son, leaped out in front of him. "Arrgh!!" Look out you stupid little kid" Billy snarled.

ARRRGH

Trying to avoid hitting Billy, Tyler ran off the sidewalk into a bush. Climbing out of the shrub, Tyler wiped moisture off his face. Seeing blood, he then realized that his already loose front tooth had been completely knocked out. "Look what you did!" he screamed at Billy. "Now I'll never win and it's all your fault!"

“So what, I’m going to win anyway. I can whistle rings around you, plus I’m older than you” Billy laughed.

“You’re only seven, BIG DEAL!”

“It’s a big deal since you can’t whistle now,” Billy laughed.

MY
TOOTH!

"I'll still beat you Billy" Tyler said defiantly. "You just wait and see!" Still the loss of that tooth, did cause Tyler to doubt himself. How could he ever win now?

TYLER
YOU LOSE!
WAIT......
YOU WIN!

That night his dreams were mixed with winning and losing.

As he dressed on the morning of the big event, he tried whistling to reassure himself that he could still compete. The sound he heard was different, but it didn't sound bad.

"Mom, are you ready?"

"Yes Tyler, I just want to pack a few snacks in case you get hungry."

"Mom, do you think I still might be able to win?" Looking into his face etched in doubts, she hugged him tightly and smiled saying, "You just do your best. Win or lose, I'll still be proud of you."

A large crowd was gathered in the park around the bandstand which was to serve as center stage for the competition. Tyler made his way to the line for his age group as they would lead the competition. As Tyler stood waiting for his turn, Billy Carp stepped in front of him. "What are you doing here?" Billy sniped. "You know you can't win."

"You don't think you're going home with any prizes do you Carpie?" Brandon's voice broke in. "Everyone knows what you did to Tyler. In fact, I think I should even the score right now." Brandon turned scowling as the color drained from Billy's face. Suddenly Brandon growled and Billy was gone in a flash.

"He won't bother you now, Tyler," Brandon laughed. "Good Luck!"

WHISTLING
CONTEST

As Tyler watched Brandon disappear into the crowd, the voice over the loudspeaker rang in his ears. "Tyler James, center stage please."

Preparing to do his song, he could feel his body going numb. He choose to do, 'Somewhere Over The Rainbow'. The only problem had been the high notes. Breathing deep, he began to whistle. As he started to relax, he noticed he was suddenly able to reach those high notes. Not only had his range increased, but there seemed to be a slight vibrato.

As he blew his last note, the hush that had fallen over the crowd broke into a rousing applause. Knowing he had done his best, Tyler proudly bowed and left the stage.

"Wow!" Brandon greeted him. "I knew you could do it."

Walking to his mom, he beamed from ear to ear. "Tyler, you were wonderful," his mother said hugging him close. "I only tried to do my best, like you said."

After all three age groups had finished, with the exception of Billy Carp, who was too scared to compete, the judges now had to decide the winners. Sandy Wilson won the11-12 group; Susan King, the 8-10 group; and Tyler James, the 5-7 group. As they went to receive their First Place Whistles, the judges were to then determine who of the three would become the Grand Prize Winner.

GRAND PRIZE
$50.00

After much consideration the judges announced the overall winner. "And our Grand Prize Winner is…..Tyler James!"

Although Tyler was thrilled to win the $50.00 gift card, it was that silver whistle he cherished the most. As he and his mother walked home, Billy stepped out in front of them.

Looking at his feet with his hands pushed deep into his pockets, Billy softly spoke, "I'm sorry that I scared you yesterday. My dad took my bike away for two weeks because of what I did to you."

Feeling Billy had already suffered enough in that he didn't even compete, Tyler extended his hand toward him. "It's alright Billy. In fact, if it hadn't been for you and losing that tooth, I might not have won the contest. So I guess I should really thank you."

As Billy reached for Tyler's hand, he noticed something was in it. In Tyler's hand was a shiny silver whistle. "You want to try my new whistle Billy?"

Walking together, a new friendship was just beginning.